# Through The Eye Of A Needle

## THE SPIRITUAL COACH™

authorHOUSE™

1663 LIBERTY DRIVE, SUITE 200
BLOOMINGTON, INDIANA 47403
(800) 839-8640
WWW.AUTHORHOUSE.COM

The Spiritual Coach Program

# THROUGH THE

# EYE OF A

# NEEDLE

*Discovering the Joy, Happiness and Freedom that Lie Beyond Material Success*

*By:* Stan Sanderson

First Edition – 2006

The Spiritual Coach
55 Museum Drive, # 608
Orillia, Ontario, Canada, L3V 7T9

Website: www.thespiritualcoach.net
Email: administration@thespiritualcoach.net

First published by AuthorHouse 3/20/2006

ISBN: 1-4208-6032-1 (dj)


Library of Congress Control Number: 2005905027

Printed in the United States of America
Bloomington, Indiana

This book is printed on acid-free paper.

*"When you find out who you really are,*
*you'll find what you've been looking for!"*

# TABLE OF CONTENTS

# ACKNOWLEDGEMENTS

I would like to express my love and gratitude to the many people without whom The Spiritual Coach Program would never have been developed, nor this book written.

First, to my dear wife, Elizabeth, who has been at my side for over fifty years, and who both loved and supported me through my many missteps in our life journey.

Second, to my four children and their lovely families, who have shown the grace to allow their dad to lecture on how one should lead their life, until he finally learned the lesson. And special thanks to my youngest son, David, for encouraging me to "follow my passion," and for his assistance in the editing process.

I am also deeply grateful to my nephew, Garner Ransom, and his company, Crux Design Group, for their untiring efforts and co-operation in creating all of our graphics, including the book cover and website. His collaboration and insights, as to approach and presentation, were invaluable.

These acknowledgements would certainly be incomplete without an attempt to mention some of the many writers and practitioners of spiritual life, who have shared their experience with me and contributed to my spiritual awakening. This includes such enlightened teachers and authors as Maurice Bucke, William James, Kahlil Gibran, Emmet Fox, Carl Yung, C. S. Lewis, T. S. Eliot, Bill Wilson, Joseph Campbell and Helen Schucman. They are no longer physically present, but their spirit and contributions live on.

It also includes contemporary seekers, teachers, authors and scholars, such as Maharishi Mahesh Yogi, M. Scott Peck, Deepak Chopra, Wayne Dyer, Paul Ferrini, Eckhart Tolle and Tom Harpur. Each one individually shining their light upon the path, while collectively providing a "beacon of hope."

In addition, I am indebted to Burt Harding who, through sharing his writings and satsang scripts, published by The Awareness Foundation, continues to remind me of the importance of "being" here-now.

# Part I.

# INTRODUCTION

# COACH'S
# SPIRITUAL AWAKENING

I recall sitting in a restaurant one night, with a very good friend, discussing the meaning of life and whether it was really *worth the candle*. He asked me, "What is the one thing you want in life, more than anything else?" After much thought I told him that what I really wanted, more than anything else in the world, was to be *happy*. He then asked, "Would it matter what you had if you were truly happy?" Obviously the answer was no. If you're happy, you're happy! How could it matter what you have?

Through this rather simple exchange, I finally realized that what I was *really* searching for was happiness, not career accomplishment and a bigger pile of "stuff," hoping that acquiring it would somehow make me happy. It had not done so in the past, and I had no reason to believe that it would do so in the future. What was required, was that I seek happiness at its Source, and not through the acquisition of *things*.

Shortly after this insight, it was suggested to me that, in order to find the *true* source of happiness, I would need to look to God, and to turn my will and my life over to his care, *as I understood him.* However, the problem with that was that I didn't know what either my *will* or my *life* were really all about, nor did I have any *workable* understanding of God. And, it was not at all clear to me just exactly how developing a closer relationship with him would provide the happiness I sought. Obviously, some very specific inquiries needed to be made.

This was made all the more difficult, because, although I was brought up in a Christian environment, and therefore my early exposure was towards Jesus and the principles attributed to him, I tended to stay clear of anything that "smacked" of religion. I didn't see myself going to Africa to save natives, or handing out pamphlets on street corners. I saw myself more as a gentleman of leisure, driving to Florida in a convertible, with the top down, a pretty woman by my side and my golf clubs in the trunk. I believed that God took care of heaven and I took care of everything down here!

It wasn't long before my search for an understanding of God, led me to a *life-changing* discovery. That there was a Power greater than me at work in the universe, and that experiencing the joy, happiness and freedom, which I had been endowed with from the beginning, was contingent *only* upon *awakening* to my spiritual reality.

This, in turn, led me to study the techniques of Transcendental Meditation, as taught by Maharishi Mahesh Yogi, through the International Meditation Society. Soon after beginning the practice of meditation, I experienced a wonderful calming effect in both my demeanor and in my physical well being. I seemed to intuitively know what to do in situations that used to baffle me, and my whole attitude and outlook on life changed for the better. Truly remarkable!

I was also blessed to have discovered a book entitled, "A Course In Miracles," published by The Foundation For Inner Peace, which confirmed my personal experience and helped to inform my universal spiritual principles. It teaches that we are all inter-connected as One, yet we see ourselves as separated individuals, living life through our own *perception*, rather than in the *reality* given to us in the beginning directly from God. Its principal thesis is that we are all the Son of God, our mission is happiness, our function is forgiveness, and *our inheritance is joy and peace*. It's a message that really speaks to my heart, and I've fully embraced these principles in my daily living.

More recently, I had the opportunity of reading Deepak Chopra's new book entitled, "How To Know God." It's a remarkable presentation of how we can actually experience the reality of God, rather than simply know *about* him. There is no question in my mind that Deepak's mission is to remind us that the spiritual truths of earlier times are equally true today, and that they will always be true. He does this through blending our spiritual reality with contemporary scientific understanding, in a way that confirms the omnipresence, omnipotence and omniscience of God in our everyday life.

Perhaps the single most important function that the God of my understanding is charged with, is allowing me to *experience* the joy, happiness and freedom which he endowed me with in the beginning. Our "arrangement," in every situation, is that I'm in charge of *inputs* and he's in charge of *outcomes*. I know that he goes before me and prepares the way, and that he can open "doors" I don't even know are there. It only remains for me to follow in faith, and to do the best that I can, with what I have, with whatever he puts in front of me. And, just so long as I continue to enjoy the fullness of my endowment, he controls the game!

Today, I am blessed with the *knowing-feeling* of joy, happiness and freedom in all that I do, regardless of the situation in which I find myself. I know who I am, where I came from and where I'm going. I now have the inner peace and sense of personal fulfilment that had been so elusive. I feel as though I'm standing on a rock, comfortable in the presence of all others, and confident in the knowledge that I belong. I have the love of my wife and family and the respect of my friends and colleagues. I enjoy perfect health, and when I put my head down at night I sleep soundly.

There is absolutely no question in my mind, that what I've experienced through my *search* for happiness, is what is called a "spiritual awakening." I have *awakened* from what I think is best described as a "sleep," in which my life was being lived through my ego-self; directed by my *conditioned mind;* responding to everything that I *perceived* as happening in my world. It's not a *complete* awakening, as I believe that when that happens I will be moving on from my human existence. However, what I have feels great! It fills my life with joy, happiness and freedom. And, since I've always been a pleasure seeker, and my awakening brings me so much pleasure every day, and throughout the day, I'll continue to do the best I can with whatever my God puts in front of me, and accept the resulting outcome. He has never let me down, and his remarkable capabilities never cease to *amaze* me!

It is my sincerest wish that you too enjoy these blessings. If you do, you know just how incredible they are, and you should continue doing whatever it is that you're doing. If you don't, then change *something*. And, if you're not sure what to change, I encourage you to define the God of your personal understanding, and to let him help you discover who you really are. *For just as soon as you find out who you really are, you'll find what you've been looking for!* The Spiritual Coach Program was created specifically to help you with that discovery.

Stan Sanderson

February, 2006

# GOD, RELIGION
# AND GENDER

God is *not* religion! And religion isn't necessary for spiritual awareness. Ironically, it is often the very thing that impedes personal spiritual experience. As God does not follow any one religion, he welcomes all religions, or none.

When the word God is used throughout The Spiritual Coach Program, the reference is to the Prime Source, First Cause or Whatever/Whomever is deemed to be the Creator of all things (see Glossary of Terms). It is not meant to be associated with any particular form of organized religion. As a matter of fact, the Second Concept of the program requires that each participant define and choose the God of his or her *own* understanding.

The program tends to emphasize universal spiritual themes rather than religious doctrine or theory. However, as I was born into a Christian environment, it follows that many of the expressions used were taken from Christian teachings. Such expressions are thought to be universal in concept and resonate with any, and all, religious teachings that espouse a similar experience.

9

It is my belief that the substance of the stories ascribed to Horus, Jesus, Moses, Mohammed, Krishna and Buddha, to mention only a few of the great icons and teachers, was informed by the same *Reality*. It would add nothing to this program to try to rationalize the differences, definitions, or religious interpretations of competing beliefs, rather than simply accept the universality of the spiritual ideas being expressed. They all lead to God in the end.

Most historical spiritual and religious writings refer to God in the male gender (he, him, his and son). While it is clear to me that the magnitude of God is inclusive of, and greatly transcends, all gender considerations, the program uses the historical male reference throughout. I hope and trust that readers and participants will allow this traditional adherence in the spirit of simplicity in the presentation.

You will also notice that I have used the corporate "we" throughout the text of The Spiritual Coach Program, rather than personal pronouns. This more accurately reflects the contributions of both thoughts and experience shared with me by so many others that have travelled the same path.

# Part II.


# THE SPIRITUAL COACH PROGRAM

# SPIRITUAL COACHING

On his deathbed, Buddha begged his disciples, "Do not accept what you hear by report, do not accept tradition, do not accept a statement because it is found in our books, nor because it is in accord with your belief, nor because it is the saying of your teacher. Be lamps unto yourselves."

What an absolutely perfect segue into the concept and practice of Spiritual Coaching. It not only takes the focus off the Coach, but makes clear wherein lies the responsibility for personal achievement. There is nothing that the most singularly skilled Coach, practicing all of the discipline at his command, can do for someone that will transcend what he or she will not do for themselves!

Many things happen when we look to a Coach for guidance. But the five most important are: we take ourselves more seriously; we take more efficient and focused actions immediately; we stop putting up with what's dragging us down; we create momentum so it's easier to get results; and, we set more focused goals than we might have without a Coach.

We engage a Spiritual Coach because we want to experience joy, happiness and freedom in our daily life; we want inner-peace and fulfilment; and, we want the path clearly defined. It's as simple as that. A Spiritual Coach helps us achieve all three more quickly.

The major differences between a Priest, a Guru and a Spiritual Coach are aptly described using the metaphor of learning to ride a bicycle all over again, after a particularly bad fall. A Priest would point out your sin in causing the fall, have you atone for your sin by washing the Bike once a week, and pray that you will be allowed to ride the Bike again in the *hereafter!* The Guru would help you to understand that the fall never really happened, the Bike is nothing, you are nothing, everything that *is* is nothing, and that there is no need to do anything to enjoy the fullness of *being* with the Bike in the *here-now!* The Spiritual Coach simply tells you to get on the Bike, runs along beside you until you're well under way, and then you don't need him anymore!

As Deepak Chopra said in his recent book, "The ultimate promise of Spirituality is to become the author of your own existence." This is not unlike what Buddha said to his disciples.

# OBJECTIVES
# OF THE PROGRAM

It has been said, "There are many gates to the Garden, but the gates are *not* the Garden." The Spiritual Coach Program is *just another gate.* Your only need for this program is if you are not yet in the Garden and wish to enter through *this* gate. The Garden of course is a metaphor for what is referred to as, "the Kingdom of God." One great teaching admonishes us, "Seek you first the Kingdom of God, and his righteousness, and all these things will be added unto you."

This begs the question, "All what things?" The reference is to the provision of everything that we will ever need. The list, in its entirety, is descriptive of the provision, protection and perfection that God conferred on each and every one of us in our *reality* as his Son.

Of particular interest to us are the blessings of joy, happiness and freedom. The fruits of which have been noticeably missing from what could be termed, "*an otherwise successful life.*" Fortunately for us, these blessings can't be separated out from the others. It's a "packaged deal." So, in finding out who we really are, we'll not only find joy, happiness and freedom, but also *uncover* a host of other blessings which were meant for our continued enjoyment.

The Spiritual Coach Program was created to serve as *another* gate to the Garden. Particularly for *otherwise successful people* who share the additional burden expressed in the proverb, "It is easier for a camel to pass through the eye of a needle, than for a rich man to enter the Kingdom of God." The reference is to someone who persists in seeking the "Kingdom" through acquired wealth, powered by his or her own abilities and personal resources.

The *bad news* is its not going to happen! The *good news*, which many have discovered, is that with God there are no degrees of difficulty. It is equally possible for both the rich man and the poor man to enter the Kingdom. The operative phrase is, *"with God."*

Once this is understood, the objective becomes crystal clear. Define the God of your personal understanding and let him help you to discover who you *really* are. With that discovery, the gate will "open" and you'll have found what you've been looking for!

# HOW IT WORKS

The Spiritual Coach Program is a simple program, consisting of Seven Concepts and Seven Strategies which, when approached as a spiritual journey, allow *otherwise successful people* to discover the joy, happiness and freedom that lie *beyond* material success. It assumes that each individual is committed to the objective, and is willing to accept some fundamental changes in his or her approach to everyday life.

The choice of using Concepts as the vehicle to briefly outline the scope of each principle was deliberate. It allows the subject to be addressed in a *directional* way, without attempting to provide all of the answers. Experience has shown that, even when the objective is the same, we do not all seek with the same level of detail or intensity. It is therefore left to each participant to explore the particular Concept in whichever way best suits his or her personal approach.

Before any progress can be made in solving a perceived problem, we must first identify the problem and determine its relative significance in our life. The First Concept in the program requires that we acknowledge and accept the fact that sustainable joy, happiness and freedom are *not* by-products of either career accomplishment or the *acquisition* of anything. Our expectation that they were was the key factor in our continued disappointment.

Once we're clear on the fundamental source of our problem, we must reassess our previous strategy and explore alternative courses of action. This eventually, and understandably, leads us to the consideration of God. In the Second Concept, we *define* our God and determine the extent of his capabilities. Our insistence is that he is able to deliver the joy, happiness and freedom we seek. We must be sure to empower him in accordance with our needs, as he can only accomplish that which we will *allow* him to do!

Immediately upon defining and choosing our God, we put him to work on our behalf. The Third Concept requires that we make a decision to allow him to take the *lead* role in our life. Not an easy task, but one of paramount importance if progress is to be made. We see the problem. There is a solution. Now is the time to change direction. Engaging God's awesome power to accomplish our objectives is an exciting prospect!

The Fourth Concept requires that we review our behavior patterns and past performances to find out what really makes us "tick." We look at ourselves objectively, perhaps for the first time, and allow ourselves to make new decisions about future actions. It's remarkable how good it makes us feel to have spent the time, and to have made the effort, to "clean house."

Just as the Fourth Concept allowed us to discover any number of personal behavior problems, or situations in need of correction, the Fifth Concept presents us with an opportunity to make any reparations that may be necessary. We also come to know that by forgiving the mistakes of others, we too are forgiven. Once this process is completed, we sense the lifting of a tremendous weight from our shoulders, and begin to experience what freedom really feels like!

# THE SPIRITUAL COACH PROGRAM

The Sixth Concept allows us to establish conscious contact with God through the use of prayer and meditation. These communication techniques are essential to discovering our true potential, and to experiencing successful outcomes in all that we do, with effortless ease. God seems to go before us to prepare the way, and opens "doors" that we didn't even know were there!

And finally, having been thorough in our approach to the preceding Concepts, the Seventh Concept confirms our ability to enjoy both our material success and the joy, happiness and freedom discovered through awareness of our spiritual reality. We recognize that God is doing for us what we were unable to do for ourselves. And, having had a *spiritual awakening* as the result of this journey, we try to carry *this* message to others, and to practice these principles in all our affairs.

It is suggested that you work through the Concepts in numerical order, using the Seven Strategies to assist you in personalizing the process. The program is not meant to be learned by rote and discussed intellectually. It is *experiential* in nature, with progress made in one Concept leading to a better appreciation and readiness to experience the next, and so on. Each participant proceeds at his or her own pace, recognizing that the objective is not to *finish* the program, but rather to *awaken* to your spiritual reality, and to savour the fruits of the journey.

After starting the program, you are encouraged to immediately begin applying and practicing your newly acquired insights in your daily activities. Subsequently, through continued practice of the program, you'll discover the joy, happiness and freedom that lie beyond material success, and make a quantum leap in your enjoyment of life.

# Part III.

# THE SEVEN CONCEPTS

# First Concept
# THE BIG LIE

The real goal of anyone pursuing career and material success, is to experience the joy, happiness and freedom which these successes *promise* to bring to his or her daily life. Most all of us have bought into the idea that a *successful* career, and the acquisition of *things*, will allow us to live happily ever after!

The problem is, it doesn't work. It never has, and it never will. It's what we call, "The Big Lie." The reason it doesn't work, quite simply, is that happiness is not a by-product of the *acquisition* of anything. It therefore follows that no level of business or career accomplishment, no matter how grandiose the title, nor any amount of material success, will bring the joy, happiness and freedom we seek.

Belief in The Big Lie is a phenomenon that is experienced by most people in the developed world. We see evidence everywhere of both its presence and the devastating affects it has had on so many lives. Probably seen most dramatically in the increased number of substance abuse problems and reported suicides among the rich and famous. Many of who were thought to have *everything* yet lived an empty existence.

Although, upon reflection, we may well feel that the poorest amongst us are those who do not attempt to "escape," and are simply disillusioned by the absence of fulfilment, approaching each day with a sense of boredom and futility.

Searching for happiness in the wrong places is perhaps one of our biggest mistakes. And will continue to be, until we discover the true nature of happiness and embrace it in our personal life. Our ladder is leaning against the wrong building. Even as we reach the top of the ladder, we're not where we want to be!

Our Creator endowed us with perfect joy, happiness and freedom at the outset, which we have somehow forgotten. Instead of seeking to achieve personal fulfilment through acquiring an ever-increasing number of *outside* things, we need only look *inside* and discover who we really are.

It's been said, "If we were to run out of things to acquire, we'd have to look at ourselves!" This would prevent our ego-self from playing the "Seek and do not find" game; focus our attention on knowing who we really are; and allow us to benefit from the "Seek and you shall find" promise.

A new awareness is required. To experience the joy, happiness and freedom we seek, we must recognize this flawed strategy and decide on a new course of action.

# *Moment of Reflection*

# "The Big Lie"

**Underlying Principle:** AWARENESS n. knowledge of a situation or fact.

**Implicit Question:** Am I aware that my "ladder," which was meant to lead me to personal fulfilment, has been leaning against the wrong building?

**Personal Discovery:** Exactly what is it that allows me to believe that additional career or material success will provide the happiness I'm seeking? Why has it not yet happened?

**Related Thought:** "Success is full of promise until you get it, then it is as last year's nest, from which the bird has flown." – H. W. Beecher (1813-1887)

# Second Concept
# THE GOD THING

Having come to the realization that happiness is not *found* in career or material success, we need to look elsewhere. And that *elsewhere* will eventually, and understandably, lead us to God. This means we are going to have to talk about the God "thing," but perhaps in a way that you may not have previously considered!

The problem is that a high percentage of *otherwise successful people* have virtually no *personal* relationship with God. There seems to be a direct correlation between the pursuit of business or professional success, and the *absence* of any personal relationship with God. The commitment we made to "improving" our life, through the acquisition of things, didn't allow much time for the development of such a relationship. It's not that we don't *believe* it's just that we don't know him all that well.

Anyone can begin to develop a personal relationship with God, simply by answering two questions, "Who is he?" and, "What can he do for me?" As to the first question, he is, and can only be, exactly what each one of us, individually, want him to be. We get to decide. There is no spiritual requirement that any of us must accept somebody else's God to be our own. We're completely free to figure out for ourselves who our God will be. In fact, our relationship with God, as each one of us understands him, is personal, and has nothing to do with Whomever, or Whatever, somebody else's God may be!

As to the second question, most of us would agree that, by any definition, God would have to be all-powerful, all-knowing, and always present, in addition to being both compassionate and merciful. However, our primary interest is that he can provide us with *sustainable* joy, happiness and freedom each and every day of our life. This has to be the test, and is the principal objective to which we are fully committed.

We need to undertake the *recruitment* of our own God. And, in so doing, we must make sure that he possesses all of the characteristics necessary to achieve our stated goals. No one needs God in his or her life to be miserable or just "fine." We're quite capable of doing that on our own. His invitation to join us will be contingent on his ability to help us discover the joy, happiness and freedom we seek.

# Moment of Reflection

## "The God Thing"

**Underlying Principle:** ACCEPTANCE n. the act of willingly accepting something offered or proposed.

**Implicit Question:** Am I willing to accept the idea of a personal relationship with God?

**Personal Discovery:** If I were to describe my current relationship with God to a close friend, what might that sound like?

**Related Thought:** "The more we let God take us over, the more truly ourselves we become – because he made us."
- C. S. Lewis (1898-1963)

# Third Concept
# THE POWER SHIFT

$N$ow that we have chosen our God, and endowed him with some impressive attributes, what do we do with him? Put him to work! Extend an invitation to him to participate in our daily life. Only by doing this are we able to employ all of his power towards the accomplishment of our objectives. We call this, "The Power Shift."

The problem most of us have with accepting God into our life, is that we might become too altruistic and have to give up some of our "stuff." Truth-be-told, a very high percentage of us have an underlying fear that to be into the God "thing" equates to denying ourselves the "good life." This has not been seen as a user-friendly idea, when to most of us the "good life" was our primary goal!

We are standing at a crossroad. A decision is required. If we decide to go straight ahead, using only our own resources, we can anticipate more of the same. On the other hand, if we decide to change direction, and rely on the power of God's resources, we open up the possibility of a whole new experience. The sole purpose of coming this far was to decide which direction we will take now. The way we came no longer matters. Its purpose was to bring us to where we currently find ourselves.

There is much to celebrate, in that we have achieved a number of material successes. On the other hand, we feel bereft of any *real* joy and happiness from these same successes. The question is simply this, "Do we want more of the same, or do we want to be happy?"

This is the decision we are confronted with. Upon our answer rests our joy, happiness and freedom in life. It is surely a decision not to be taken lightly, nor to be put off until some future time. We see the problem. There is a solution. Now is the time to change direction.

Once we decide in favor of happiness, we delegate complete operating authority to God. He is now free to add his expertise and resources to everything that we do. All that is required of us, is to believe that he can provide the joy, happiness and freedom we seek, and that we're *willing* to cooperate in the process. Trust him, and watch what happens!

# Moment of Reflection

## "The Power Shift"

**Underlying Principle:** COMMITMENT n. the act or process of entrusting or consigning; the state of being committed; an engagement or pledge to do something.

**Implicit Question:** Am I prepared to extend an invitation to the God of my understanding, to actively participate in my life?

**Personal Discovery:** Because I've stood at this very same crossroad before, and *not* changed direction, why do I think that this time will be different?

**Related Thought:** "In the many adversities and trials of life it is often hard to say 'Thy will be done.' But why not say it? God ever does only what is right and wise and best; what is prompted by a father's love, and what to his children will work out to their highest good." – Edward Payson (1783-1827)

# Fourth Concept
# THE RENOVATION PROCESS

Our invitation to God to join with us in our daily life requires that we review the condition of the "house" we will be sharing. To the extent that we have unfinished projects, shoddy maintenance and some rather old furnishings, we would certainly want to renovate before he takes up residence. We'd also feel much better about the potential effectiveness of our new relationship if our house was in order. This we call, "The Renovation Process."

The problem facing most programs of personal renewal, is the high incidence of relapse. Our attempts at New Year's resolutions are a classic example of the high failure rate among participants. Albeit that we start with the best of intentions. The difference between those resolutions and what we're doing in this renovation process, is the high risk associated with our failure. We have been denied our reasonable share of joy, happiness and freedom for far too long, and are not in any way prepared to jeopardize our present and future participation.

As with any renovation program, not all of what is inspected requires repair or replacement. We often find that a significant percentage of what is examined is in very good condition and worthy of retention. These are not the things that give us cause for concern. It is the frayed or faulty wiring, which is capable of short circuiting our best-laid plans, that is most in need of repair. We must also look very carefully at the structural support mechanisms, which, if in a weakened condition, could result in an untimely collapse.

We need to review our past performances to find out what really makes us "tick." Our inspection will be thorough and searching, for as Plato said, "The unexamined life is not worth living." Here we examine our life to find out why we are "wired" to act in certain ways. We will look at ourselves objectively, perhaps for the first time, and allow ourselves to make new decisions about future actions. How have we been shaped by major events in our life, and do we find that acceptable?

It's remarkable how good it makes us feel to have spent the time, and to have made the effort, to "clean house." Unlike spring cleaning, this renovation process is not an annual event. Once completed, and our corrections made, it should not be necessary to repeat it in the foreseeable future. We will have made a pile of all that we no longer wish to hold onto, and taken it to the dumpster. It's an exhilarating feeling!

# *Moment of Reflection*

## "The Renovation Process"

**Underlying Principle:** REPARATIONS n. the act of making amends; atonement; repairing or the state of being repaired.

**Implicit Question:** Am I willing to critically examine my past behaviour pattern, to uncover any errors which may be in need of correction?

**Personal Discovery:** Do I persist in holding on to my old ideas, expecting to achieve a different result?

**Related Thought:** "We ought not to look back unless it is to derive useful lessons from past errors, and for the purpose of profiting from our dearly bought experience."
- George Washington (1732-1799)

# Fifth Concept
# THE RELEASE FACTOR

Having taken an objective look at ourselves, we have probably found a number of things that are in need of correction. We may also have discovered things that we had done to others for which we should consider making amends. In fact, truth-be-told, we would appreciate the opportunity to correct these *errors* and to offer the appropriate amends to make things right.

Unresolved errors leave us with guilt feelings, to a greater or lesser degree, depending on the seriousness of the issue. The only way to be released from these guilt feelings is to recognize the *whole truth* of the situation, and make whatever reparations are necessary.

We tend to have a real problem with the idea of forgiveness. Not so much with forgiving others, as we *say* we're always willing to do, but in seeking, and accepting, forgiveness for ourselves. Even to the point of living with the guilt as the lesser of two "evils." Maybe someday we will get to fix things up and feel better about ourselves. After all, we rationalize, a lot of people have done things to us for which they've never made amends. Unfortunately, this type of rationalization does not relieve our gnawing guilt feelings. So, unless we deal with the *cause* of these feelings, we'll have no choice but to continue to live with them.

We are fortunate indeed, that our being forgiven is not contingent on the "injured" party forgiving us! According to the "Law of Giving," to the extent that we offer forgiveness to others, for all of their errors, we will receive it for ourselves. This law is also confirmed in the Lord's Prayer, "Forgive us our trespasses as we forgive those who trespass against us." We will come to know, however, that the forgiveness we offer to others must be *total* and from the *heart*, if we are to receive meaningful forgiveness for ourselves. We call this, "The Release Factor."

There is an incredible feeling of release experienced through the total forgiveness of others. Within a relatively short period of time, following our forgiveness of others, we will recognize that we too have been forgiven. We sense the lifting of a tremendous weight from our shoulders, and begin to experience what freedom really feels like. Incredible indeed!

# *Moment of Reflection*

## "The Release Factor"

**Underlying Principle:** FORGIVENESS n. the act of forgiving or the state of being forgiven.

**Implicit Question:** Am I prepared to forgive *all* others for the wrongs which I *believe* have been done to me?

**Personal Discovery:** When I tell my "side" of the story, is that *really* what happened, or is it just what I'd like others to *think* happened? How might it sound if I were more *honest* about *my* needs?

**Related Thought:** "It is in vain for you to expect, and it is impudent for you to ask, of God, forgiveness for yourself, if you refuse to exercise this forgiving temper as to others." – Benjamin Hoadley (1676-1761)

# Sixth Concept
# THE DIRECT CONNECTION

If we have been thorough in our renovation and forgiveness efforts, we begin to notice a change in ourselves. We have a new feeling of inner peace, and can sense the true potential of a life lived with, and directed by, the God of our understanding. Actually, we've been preparing ourselves for something which is truly remarkable: *Conscious contact with God!*

The good news is that conscious contact with God is achievable. In fact, it is one of the most natural abilities available to us, given our direct descendents. The bad news is we either don't know it, or haven't developed the skills required to communicate with him directly. Conscious contact with God allows us to discover our true potential, and to create successful outcomes and good fortune with effortless ease. We call this, "The Direct Connection."

The problem is that we're using *conditioned responses* to deal with the events of the day, rather than bringing them to God and asking for direction. God wants us to have everything our heart desires. In fact, all of his

43

phenomenal resources are consistently applied to just that purpose. The only thing that prevents the realization of our desires is our *other* agenda. Often kept secret from our own conscious awareness, and definitely from God's.

When we bring everything to God, and seek his direction, we shine a light on the entire subject matter and position ourselves to experience the best possible outcome. It is now time to let go of our old ideas and allow God to enter our heart and life, as we have never before imagined.

Just how do we do this, contact God directly? Actually, it's quite simple; the tools we use are prayer and meditation. Prayer is *talking* to God, and meditation is *listening*. We need to set aside a specific time each morning for this important communication. It's a very small *investment* of time that will pay huge dividends as our day progresses.

Establishing conscious contact with God has a profound effect on our everyday confidence and enthusiasm for life. It's not long before we begin to see that things seem to work out better than they used to. People appear to be more understanding and our enjoyment of life is greatly enhanced. God seems to go before us and prepare the way. And, he opens doors we didn't even know were there. With results like this, our morning communication is *imperative!*

# Moment of Reflection

## "The Direct Connection"

**Underlying Principle:** KNOWLEDGE n. information or awareness acquired through experience or education; deep and extensive learning; the sum of what is known.

**Implicit Question:** Am I confident that I know where to go; what to do; what to say; and who to say it to?

**Personal Discovery:** If I'm not relying on the "Source" of *all* knowledge for guidance and direction, to *what* am I entrusting my life?

**Related Thought:** "The wise man is but a clever infant, spelling letters from a hieroglyphical prophetic book, the lexicon of which lies in eternity." - Thomas Carlyle (1795-1881)

# Seventh Concept
## THE 200% LIFE

We began with the realization that no amount of career or material success could ever bring us the joy, happiness and freedom we sought. We've come a long way. We defined our God, invited him to join in our life, and empowered him to act on our behalf. Took a personal inventory of ourselves, made reparations where necessary, and received forgiveness through extending it to others. We established a morning routine, which includes both prayer and meditation, enabling us to make conscious contact with God for daily guidance and direction.

Each one of these Concepts was essential to discovering the 100% of our spiritual reality that provides us with the joy of life. And, when this is added to the 100% of our material life, we begin to experience what we call, "The 200% Life."

There is no lack of joy, happiness and freedom, nor any scarcity of resources, in a life lived with God and guided by spiritual principles. It allows us to have, and enjoy, both happiness and material success at the same time, each on its own level. This was our real goal from the beginning, and its achievement is now clearly in sight.

As we live The 200% Life, our whole attitude and outlook on life will change. We will experience joy, happiness and freedom in our daily life, and know inner peace. That awful gut feeling that *something is missing* will leave us. We will intuitively know how to handle situations that used to baffle us. The enjoyment of our material success will be greatly enhanced, not only for us, but also for our loved ones. We will enjoy the benefit of an unlimited supply of *all* that we desire, and recognize that God is doing for us what we were unable to do for ourselves.

Having had a *spiritual awakening* as the result of this journey, we try to carry *this* message to others, and to practice these principles in all our affairs.

# *Moment of Reflection*

## "The 200% Life"

**Underlying Principle:** FULFILMENT n. satisfaction resulting from fully developing ones abilities; the accomplishment of something promised.

**Implicit Question:** Am I enjoying the presence of everything that my *heart* desires?

**Personal Discovery:** If the "hose that waters the garden" is not *flowing* to its full potential, could it be that I have my "foot" on it?

**Related Thought:** "Plenty and indigence depend upon the *opinion* everyone has of them; and riches, like glory or health, have no more beauty or pleasure, than their possessor is pleased to lend them." – Michel E. de Montaigne (1533-1592)

# Part IV.

# THE SEVEN STRATEGIES

# First Strategy
# KNOW YOURSELF

One of the greatest questions of all time is "Who are you?" Many of us respond with our name, job title and place of work. Which is what we do, *not* who we are! While others of us will quote our name, residence and family status. Which is what we have, *not* who we are! Why is it so difficult to answer the question precisely? Because we tend to describe ourselves relative to other peoples' interest in us, or our interest in them, and not as to who we *really* are.

The problem is that few of us have any idea as to who we really are. It's often not until mid-life that we even give it much thought. We're all familiar with the successful person who tells us, "I'm taking a year off and going to Europe to find myself." It begs the question, "Who's lost?" The short answer is that no one is *lost* in God's awareness, but God has been *lost* in our awareness.

One of the misconceptions of life, is that we are human beings having a spiritual experience. When, in reality, we're spiritual beings having a human experience. Is it any wonder, then, that we become confused, frustrated and even angry, when our best human efforts and applied wisdom do not bring the satisfaction we seek. The gut feeling that *something is missing* in our life is our "Self" seeking its own identity.

When we find out who we really are, we'll find what we've been looking for! Our task is a simple one, not easy, but simple. We need to recognize our *true* identity and live life through our spiritual reality. We receive an incredible blessing when we discover the complete fulfilment that is, and always has been, our birthright. It is only when we apply spiritual principles to our human objectives that the outcomes include joy, happiness and freedom. There is one promise which we can totally rely on, "Seek and you shall find." It therefore augurs well that we are now seeking.

# *Applying the Strategy*

# "Know Yourself"

**Practical Consideration:**

- When I say that I'm a "human being," what is it that's the "human" part? What's the "being" part?

- If God were to brag about me to someone, as his favourite child, what would he say is the *phase* I'm going through? And, what would he say I'm going to *be* when I grow up?

- If God is "King" and I am his son, then it follows that I'm a "Prince," and, as such, I live in a beautiful palace and am heir to the entire "Kingdom." Why do I *choose* to live in the *basement* of the palace, clutching the few trinkets that I have at hand?

**Personal Application:**

- When I ask myself what it is about *money* that's *important* to me, what's the answer? Then, when I ask myself what it is about what I just answered, that's *important* to me, what's my answer? Continuing with this line of enquiry until I can't go any further, what's the *one* thing that's *really important* to me?

- As God made me who I am, I will stop comparing myself to other people. It's a loser's game. If, by comparison, I fall short, I'll feel *inferior*. If I come out ahead, I'll feel *superior*. Either way I lose!

- Because I'm not *really* the secular/hedonistic person I've been *masquerading* as, I'll give up my personal "story," complete with all its problems and self-protecting rationalizations, and begin anew.

**Pertinent Quotation:**

- "We shall never cease from exploration, and at the end of all exploring, we shall arrive at where we started, but *know* that place for the first time." – T. S. Eliot (1888-1965)

# Second Strategy
# CHOOSE YOUR GOD

God is *not* religion! And religion isn't necessary for spiritual awareness. Sometimes it is the very thing that impedes personal spiritual experience. As God does not follow any one religion, he welcomes all religions, or none. If your religion brings you joy, happiness and freedom, and provides the relationship you wish to have with your God, that's great. You're blessed in being counted among those who have established an effective personal relationship with the God of their choice. Many of us are not so blessed. We're working on it!

Our approach to God is by way of personal spiritual experience rather than theology. We believe that a universal theology is impossible. Whereas a universal spiritual awareness is not only possible, it is necessary to the achievement of a *common* spiritual objective, regardless of the chosen path. Therefore, we tend to emphasize universal spiritual themes rather than religious doctrine or theory.

As a wise man once said, "There are many gates to the Garden, but the gates are *not* the Garden." The good news is that each one of us gets to choose our own *gate*. And, our experience has shown that the best way to choose a *gate* is to first revisit the relationship we currently have with God, if any.

We need to ask ourselves, "Does my current God represent the God I would personally choose?" If the answer is "Yes," then we keep our existing God. However, if the answer is "No," we need to challenge ourselves to come up with a God that does! This will require that we drill down into our belief system and examine each one of our old ideas about who our God is, and consider exchanging them for who he has to be.

It's critical to our objective that the characteristics we choose are appropriate for the tasks we will be asking him to perform, as he can only do for us what we will *allow* him to do, and *nothing* more! We need to clarify precisely what it is we want God to do for us, and proclaim our faith in his ability to succeed.

This is the moment that most of us have been waiting for. No time to be timid in our requests. On the contrary, it is the precise time to express our greatest desires and wishes for our future life. We're now about to travel on the road to realization!

# *Applying the Strategy*

## "Choose Your God"

**Practical Consideration:**

- Am I prepared to develop a more meaningful relationship with the God of my understanding?

- Does my current understanding of God represent the God I would *personally* choose? If so, how so? If not, why not?

- Are the characteristics, which I ascribe to the God of my understanding, appropriate for the tasks that I will be asking him to perform?

**Personal Application:**

- Before recruiting to fill the "God" position in my life, I will prepare a job description and define the requisite qualifications.

- It is essential that I clearly articulate exactly what it is that I want God to do for me, in both the short and long term. Making a list is the most effective way to reveal my *intentions*, and to focus my *attention*.

- Once I have chosen my God, and outlined his mandate, I will meet with him privately to formally engage his services, and to establish a protocol for performance reporting.

**Pertinent Quotation:**

- "Who guides below and rules above, the great disposer and the mighty king; than he none greater; next him none can be, or is, or was; supreme, he singly fills the throne." – Horace (65 BCE - 8 CE)

# Third Strategy
# DELEGATE AUTHORITY

If our chosen God is all that we have described him as being, then it follows that we should charge him with the responsibility for performance. Applying his resources to any given situation allows a far greater potential for success and the best possible outcome. To do anything other than that, from the standpoint of logic alone, would be to assure a lesser result.

As any good manager knows, adequate authority must accompany responsibility for performance. And, therefore, it's required that we delegate full operating authority to God, as we understand him, so that he may carry out his mandate.

The problem most of us have in delegating authority, is our fear of loss of control. Our conditioned mind tends to suggest that he might not be fully aware of the history of this particular situation, and it might be better if we took over. However, we must resolve this dilemma in favor of God if we are to achieve the results hoped for. And, as we have been in the practice of "controlling" the outcomes of our activities in the past, it is not expected to be an easy adjustment to make. But make it we must! Therefore we need to be vigilant in keeping our commitment to allow our God to control the game.

If our God is both all-knowing and all-powerful, the outcome of any action must be exactly as it was supposed to be. Perchance it was not as we had anticipated, rest assured that there was a greater good being served. Something outside our current awareness, the specifics of which may never be known to us.

God has three possible answers to everything we ask of him; "Yes," "No" and "Not yet!" The answer that we tend to have the most trouble with is "Not yet." We can generally handle a "Yes" or a "No," it's the "Not yet" answer that baffles us. Instead of accepting that the time is not *right* for whatever it is to happen, we regroup and begin a new offensive to make it happen. Should we be "successful" in forcing it to happen, it could prove to be detrimental to our overall well being.

Remember, "God guides, God provides." Learning to trust God is one of the highest goals to which we can aspire. And, one of the most rewarding. Relax, and enjoy the trip.

# Applying the Strategy

## "Delegate Authority"

**Practical Consideration:**

- What fears surface when I think about turning my *complete* life over to God? What is it that I *believe* I'm better able to handle?

- Is it rational for me to believe that, with God controlling the "game," I will no longer be able to participate in what is often described as the "good life?" Might I benefit from revisiting my *definition* of the term?

- What does the maxim "God guides, God provides" suggest to me in terms of delegating authority?

**Personal Application:**

- I will re-evaluate both the *positive* and *negative* results that I've experienced through the use of what, up until now, has been the "driving force" in my life.

- It will be most helpful to me to make a list of all of the things that I'll be turning over to God. The more specific and thorough the list, the more effective it will be.

- If after one year, I'm looking back on having delegated complete operating authority to God, what are some of the things that would have had to happen for me to regard it as a success?

**Pertinent Quotation:**

- "See God on both sides of the table. Then if you don't make that sale, you'll make a *better* one instead. If you don't get the job, you'll get a *better* one. If you don't make the arrangement that you sought today, a *better* one will present itself tomorrow." - Emmet Fox (1886-1951)

# Fourth Strategy
# PERSONAL INVENTORY

Every successful business periodically takes an inventory of its merchandise. It must determine not only what is in stock, but also the condition of the goods. That which is saleable will be retained, while that which is damaged will be either repaired or discarded. The future profitability of the business depends on both the thoroughness and honesty with which the inventory is taken.

This same principle holds true for taking our personal inventory. Our *saleable* assets are our positive behavior, business acumen, inter-personal skills, intellectual understanding, good health, compassionate demeanor and our grateful attitude. While our *damaged* goods include detrimental behavior patterns, areas of poor performance, attitudinal difficulties, unresolved emotional stresses, anger and resentments. These lists are by no means exhaustive, but rather indicative of the kinds of inventory items that need to be thoroughly reviewed if we are to operate *profitably* in the future.

One of the problems we encounter in taking a personal inventory, is our tendency to blame some of our difficulties on other people. This often happens when we discover areas of dishonesty or self-seeking in our own behavior. However, as our best results will come from an honest assessment of *our* behavior, we are well advised to remember that this exercise is a *personal* inventory, and the role that others may have played is not our current concern. At best it distracts us from our desired outcome, at worst it can be misleading or harmful.

It is a spiritual axiom, that you can't solve a problem with the same mind that created it. It therefore follows that if we're to solve our behavioral problems, we will have to *change* our mind. Once we have the results of our personal inventory, we will be required to give careful consideration to each and every item in the *damaged* section, so that it can either be corrected or discarded. Either action requires that we change our mind about how we will proceed in the future. The results we achieve will be the "barometer" of our thoroughness and honesty.

Taking a personal inventory puts us in the enviable position of being able to make new choices. It is precisely these new choices that will allow us to both improve and enjoy our future performance. An examined life is indeed worth living!

# *Applying the Strategy*

## "Personal Inventory"

**Practical Consideration:**

- How many times have I caught myself exclaiming, "I can't believe I did that *again!*" Could it be the result of not having made any changes in my behaviour?

- If my God given talents have allowed me to enjoy success in my material life, why have I been so hesitant in adapting these same talents to the benefit of my personal life?

- How have I been shaped by major events in my life, and do I find that acceptable?

**Personal Application:**

- Undertaking a thorough and objective review of my past performances will help to *identify* unfavourable behaviour patterns, and point towards the changes necessary to *improve* future performance.

- I will resist the tendency to *blame* some of my difficulties on other people, particularly as I discover areas of *dishonesty* or *self-seeking* in my own behaviour, as it can be misleading or harmful to my desired outcome.

- As motivation is *always* a drive towards being better, *unconsciously* driven motivation leads to the *constant* feeling that something is *missing*. By uncovering my *hidden motivators*, there exists the possibility of experiencing a sense of *continuous* achievement.

**Pertinent Quotation:**

- "It is our own past which has made us what we are. We are the children of our own deeds. Conduct has created character; acts have grown into habits, each year has pressed into us a deeper moral print; the lives we have led have left us such as we are today." – John B. Dykes (1823-1876)

# Fifth Strategy
# FORGIVENESS

The Golden Rule is perhaps one of the most well known spiritual principles of all time. "Do unto others as you would have them do unto you." It is generally agreed that this is the appropriate way to treat other people. What is not so well known, is that it is a spiritual law (the Law of Giving) mandating that, "As you give, so shall you receive."

Therefore, if you want forgiveness, forgive others; if you want freedom, give freedom to others; if you want attention and appreciation, learn to give attention and appreciation; and, if you want material affluence, help others to become materially affluent. In fact the easiest way to get what you want, is to give it away! This "dynamic exchange" is the *automatic* effect of the Law of Giving.

Unfortunately, although most of us understand this phenomenon *intellectually*, we have not adapted it *beneficially* in our everyday life. Actually, we all too frequently use this spiritual law against ourselves by misunderstanding its full implications. When we attempt to justify the projection of guilt onto others, so that we may feel free of it, a "boomerang" effect is automatically established. We will then sense our own sinfulness, carry its guilt, and expect to be punished accordingly. And will be. It's the law! We get back in direct proportion as to what we give out. Therefore we must be very selective in what we *give* to others.

We are responsible for whatever is in our life! What wonderful news for those of us who have always sought to be in full control of our life. We were terribly upset when we thought others were responsible for what had happened to us in certain instances. However, since we are the authors of our own script, what we thought was being done to us, we actually did to ourselves. Albeit, not with conscious intent.

Given this reality, we need to forgive other people for what they *did not* do to us, not what they *did* to us! Our prayer could properly be, "God, help me to forgive all of the people for the errors that *I* have made." This correctly represents what must happen if we are responsible for writing our own script. We need to stop blaming others for outcomes that were *required* in our life!

Once we understand who writes the script we have the opportunity to positively affect every thing that we do, and everyone we come in contact with. This is perhaps the greatest single lesson we can learn in life. And, it certainly makes the discipline and effort required to learn it, well worth the candle.

# Applying the Strategy

## "Forgiveness"

**Practical Consideration:**

- Why do I find it so hard to forgive? Is it because there's a certain *justification* for *my* actions in feeling that I've been wronged?

- Given that I'm responsible for *everything* that comes into my life, how can I possibly hold other people accountable to *me* for their actions?

- If I'm to do unto others, as I would have them do unto me, how might my approach to them change if I saw each one of them as wearing a nametag - with *my* name on it?

**Personal Application:**

- I will make a list of all the people with whom I have unresolved issues. This information will assist me in determining the extent to which forgiveness may be required.

- In seeking forgiveness for something I did, which may have *harmed* someone, I will first determine *precisely* what it was that happened, and what could be done, *specifically*, to correct it. After which, I'll make the necessary amend, *directly*, at my earliest opportunity.

- At the end of each day, I will review the events of the day, to determine if there is anything for which I need to either forgive or seek forgiveness. If so, whatever correction is deemed to be necessary is to be done without delay.

**Pertinent Quotation:**

- "Retribution is one of the grand principles in the divine administration of human affairs; a requital is imperceptible only to the *wilfully* unobservant. There is everywhere the working of the everlasting law of requital: man always gets as he gives." – John Foster (1836-1917)

# Sixth Strategy
# PRAYER AND MEDITATION

Words are still the principal means of our communication, while silence is the language of the Spirit. Therefore, as we have invited God into our life, we are confronted with a communications challenge. We need to use words to speak to God, through prayer, while he uses silence to speak to us, through meditation. It is therefore crucial to our spiritual progress that we become fluently bilingual!

The trouble most of us have, is that we're not practiced in the effective use of prayer and meditation. Our prayers have generally been as supplicants, seeking favor for our current situation. This is in contra-distinction to who we really are, and our absolute birthright to the full support of all of God's resources. We need only ask for his guidance, as to what to do, and for the strength, power and ability to carry it out.

Many of us have had little or no instruction in meditative techniques. Attempts at meditation were often ineffectual, as we were unable to still our active mind. We also weren't exactly sure what we were supposed to be experiencing. This undisciplined approach made the whole process difficult, if not impossible.

We meet with God each morning to seek his guidance. This meeting takes place immediately after rising, before the pressures of the day descend upon us. We review the upcoming events, and ask for direction in all that we plan to do. Clarity of the action required comes through the use of both prayer and meditation. This process moves our words *out* and his guidance *in*. Only then are we properly prepared to meet the events of the day.

As we learn to use prayer and meditation effectively, we see how easily and effortlessly positive results are achieved. God's participation assures us that whatever we do will be fully supported from inception to completion. When we contrast this to the fact that whatever we do alone requires our continued attention and effort, we begin to understand the practical implications of the process. Increased confidence and far less anxiety are but two of the many benefits.

# *Applying the Strategy*

# "Prayer and Meditation"

**Practical Consideration:**

- Are my prayers to God only to know his will for me, and to have the strength, power and ability to carry it out? Or, do I have another agenda?

- If I agree that the *language* of the spirit is *silence*, have I been giving God enough *quiet* time to insure a reasonable measure of guidance?

- Have I noticed that the most *meaningful* moments in my life were *not* planned by me, but came easily into my awareness in response to a *heart* felt desire? Whom do I think did the planning and made all of the arrangements?

**Personal Application:**

- I will set aside a specific time each morning to meet with my God, and to seek direction for the day through both prayer and meditation

- When I speak to God in prayer, I will acknowledge each anticipated event in the day, and ask him to help me to know *his* will, and to have the strength, power and ability to carry it out.

- Before starting my meditation, I will ask God to help me to know who I *really* am, and to speak to my *heart*. And, although his response may not be immediately discernible to me, I will trust that the direction I need will subsequently become clear.

**Pertinent Quotation:**

- "There is no thought in any mind, but it quickly tends to convert itself into a power, and organizes a huge instrumentality of means." – Ralph Waldo Emerson (1803-1882)

# Seventh Strategy
# TOTAL DETACHMENT

The main reason that we seek to increase our material success is to achieve a sense of personal security. But, can the world give us security? Security is a spiritual *knowing-feeling* that can only exist when we no longer care about worldly security! Now do we wonder why spiritual enlightenment is so rare?

Just so long as we believe that our security is *contingent* upon acquiring or retaining anything, we will be subject to feelings of insecurity, no matter how great our wealth. This in no way is to suggest that we will feel insecure by acquiring or retaining anything. It simply says that if we *believe* our security is contingent on these things we will feel insecure. There is a huge difference between these two positions. It's the difference between inner peace and constant anxiety!

Seeking security through the acquisition of things is like chasing the horizon. We see it just ahead, then, as we approach, it moves a little further away. As we try again to approach it, it moves yet again. It's impossible to reach the horizon no matter how far we travel. Simply because the horizon, like the feeling of security, is not a *thing* that can be acquired, it can only be experienced.

Buddha said, "Detachment is the essence of spiritual enlightenment." Wow! Talk about knowing where to look for the root cause of our insecurities. It is a message that can lead us to the awareness of the God given inner peace that we were meant to know from the beginning. By practicing non attachment to *anything* that comes into our life, we are not only free to fully enjoy its presence, but also to never experience a sense of loss in its absence. This is a spiritual blessing that can *only* be appreciated through total detachment.

Security is a feeling that emanates from a deep and profound *knowing-feeling* that nothing we gain, or lose, has the power to affect our personal well being. The reality is that God gave us everything we would ever need to assure our security and enjoyment of life. We do not have to acquire or achieve *anything* to experience the joy, happiness and freedom that are ours. What we need is to sharpen our awareness, be open to all things, *and attached to nothing!*

# *Applying the Strategy*

# "Total Detachment"

**Practical Consideration:**

- Have I been seeking personal security through the acquisition and accumulation of material things?

- Do I now understand that security is a spiritual *knowing-feeling* that can only exist when I no longer *care* about worldly security?

- Given the true *nature* of personal security, is it clear to me as to why spiritual *enlightenment* is so rare?

**Personal Application:**

- By practising non attachment to *anything* that comes into my life, I am not only free to fully enjoy its *presence*, but also to never experience a sense of loss in its *absence*.

- The *experience* of either inner-peace or constant anxiety, is the direct result of the beliefs and priorities which I *choose* to exercise in my everyday life.

- There is *nothing* that I have to acquire, or achieve, to experience the joy, happiness and freedom that have been mine from the beginning. I need only to sharpen my awareness, be open to all things, *and attached to nothing.*

**Pertinent Quotation:**

- "A contented mind is the greatest blessing a man can enjoy in this world; and if, in the present life, his happiness arises from the subduing of his desires, it will arise in the next from the gratification of them."
  – Joseph Addison (1672-1719)

# Part V.

# STARTING EACH DAY

# MORNING COMMITMENT

The principle of the "Seven P's" is well known in the business world, "Proper pre-preparation prevents piss-poor performance!" Although the Boy Scouts perhaps said it more succinctly, and certainly more delicately, in their motto, "Be prepared." This principle is no less important for someone wanting to have a good day, regardless of what, or who, may be on his or her agenda for that day. This is particularly true when you're attempting to have a more meaningful experience from all that *happens* in your life.

Each one of us must decide for ourselves how we're going to start our day. It's the only way that we'll have any hope of sticking to the commitment we make. Naturally, your decision will be impacted by many factors. What's important to you? What results are you getting from what you're currently doing? How serious are you about effecting change in your life? How much time are you willing to commit in the morning? There is no *one* answer. However, there is one thing that is unequivocal about your morning commitment. Once you decide what you're prepared to do, *do it!* And, if it's not possible to do it first thing in the morning, do it at your first opportunity.

Maharishi Mahesh Yogi says, "It is most important to meditate immediately upon rising, after you have washed out your mouth, before the pressures of the day descend upon you." The fact is that the encounters you *require* in your life today will happen. The only variable is your *reaction* to them. The question is, "How prepared will you be to receive the best possible outcome from each situation?"

One way to enhance the results of each encounter in your day, is to select a quiet place, where you can be alone and are not likely to be disturbed, and enter into direct communication with the God of your personal understanding. Begin by speaking to him in prayer, acknowledging each anticipated event in the day. Ask that he help you to know his will in it, and to give you the strength, power and ability to carry it out.

Your prayers are then followed by your morning meditation. As you begin, ask him to help you to remember who you really are, and to "speak" to your heart. In silence, he will respond. And, although his response may not be immediately discernible to you, the message or direction you require will subsequently become clear. Trust him, and each day will be better than the day before. Your progress is assured!

One common question is, "How much time do I have to spend each morning?" Spiritual Coaches will tell you that they spend from one to two hours, or more, each and every morning. It may be that ten or fifteen minutes are all that you can do at the outset. If so, fine. But commit to it, and do it each morning without fail. You can extend the time commitment as you progress. It is truly a commitment that is both voluntary and self-monitored.

In the investment business they have something called, "Return on Investment." If investment capital is measured by the hours in a day, we each have twenty-four units of *capital* available for investment purposes. If we were to *invest* just one of those hours, first thing in the morning, towards preparing ourselves to get the maximum benefit out of the remaining twenty-three hours, our return on invested capital would be *exponential!* It's an investment well worth making.

# PRAYER

If the God of your understanding is truly engaged in representing your best interests, he isn't *only* present during your morning prayers, he is with you all of the time. This allows you to be in constant communication with him throughout the day and night. In fact, he is a devotee of the principle of "division of labour," and is best able to perform his duties, and to help you with yours, if there is regular *feedback* from you as the day progresses.

As your attention becomes focused on the magnitude of his grace and kindness, he's open to hearing a prayer of *adoration*. It helps him to know that you appreciate his compassion. This type of prayer reinforces your understanding of his considerable attributes. And, truth-be-told, it's more important for you to express your understanding than it is for him to be adored. He's teaching you, and knows you're getting it when you acknowledge an insight.

You will also become aware of how you fell short in some aspect of what you had planned to do, or how you "lost it" in a confrontation with someone. When this happens, he wants to hear your prayer of *contrition*. It's through acknowledging your shortcomings that you demonstrate that you know the right thing to do, even though you screwed up. Because, if he doesn't know that you know, you'll have to repeat the lesson. It is instructive to remember that, in Zen Buddhism, one is taught, "To know, and not to do, is not yet to know!"

With God in your life, walking beside you, each and every minute of each and every day, you will notice that you have many opportunities for prayers of *thanksgiving* for the wonderful things that he does for you. These prayers are his favorites. It shows that your heart is filled with gratitude and thankfulness for the blessings you have received. And, since he is always interested in your happiness, and you have told him exactly what pleases you, you can expect even more of these blessings. He may be God, but he still needs your *feedback!*

And, lastly, he wants to hear your prayers of *supplication*. He waits like an anxious lover, ready to supply your every need. Tell him what you want, and why you want it. Let him be the arbiter of its usefulness in helping you to awaken to the joy, happiness and freedom you seek. Only he knows the *true* value of everything you *think* you need. Eventually, as you grow in your awareness of who you really are, your prayers of supplication will narrow to praying only to know God's will for you, and to have the strength, power and ability to carry it out. His will for you includes that you live each moment of your life in the joy and peace of your inheritance. *Is there anything else that you want?*

# MEDITATION

$M$editation is perhaps the highest form of communication with God. Its primary purpose is to allow him to give you the guidance you seek *directly*, in the only "language" he knows, *silence!* Therefore, it is essential that you quell the "chatter" going on in your head so that his guidance can be "heard."

While there are any number of meditative techniques available to help you improve your communication skills, it is more important that you *begin* the practice than it is to find the *best* technique. You can begin by simply sitting comfortably, either in a chair or cross-legged on the floor, your choice, and placing your hands together in your lap. Close your eyes, and consciously relax your body from your head down to your toes, feeling the muscles letting go as you give attention to each part of your body. Then, in this relaxed condition, ask God to help you to remember who you really are, and to "speak" to your heart.

Sit quietly, allowing all thoughts to clear from your mind. They may insist on coming back, but don't fight them. As each thought comes into your mind, simply let it go. Don't focus on it, just release it, and let it go. It can be helpful if you focus on the quiet rhythm of your breathing. Allowing it to go slower and shallower with each breath, until you feel that you're hardly breathing at all. Both your breathing and your heartbeat slow considerably during meditation.

Then, introduce a word-sound (mantra), such as the popular Sanskrit word "Om," into your awareness. The word-sound itself has little or no meaning to distract you, and helps to keep other thoughts from entering your mind. The sound that you hear in your head will be "ohmmm," which resonates well with the brain, taking you further into the meditative process, and leaving the material plane behind. You will be aware of nothing at the time, but are in what is known as "the Gap." That space between consciousness and God, wherein lies *all* knowledge, and, as Deepak Chopra says, "where spiritual activity commands its own laws." It is here that God "speaks" to your heart, in silence.

As you return to the moment, you may not be aware of any great insight or revelation that you were hoping to receive. That's normal in the process. However, as you progress in the practice of meditation, you will begin to "see" things much more clearly than ever before. The greatest challenge is to stay with it. The biggest reason we don't stay with the practice of meditation, is performance anxiety. Regardless, as it is the single most important thing you'll ever do, don't allow your ego to convince you that you haven't the time to meditate, or that the process is too slow, or, even worse, that it's not working. *"Be still and know that I am God!"*

It is suggested that you allow about thirty minutes for the whole process of meditation. If you find it too difficult to keep your focus for thirty minutes, do it for as long as you can, and then just a little bit longer. It will get easier as you become more practiced in the technique and personally experience more of the benefits. Some feel that they are greatly advantaged from a second meditation in the evening.

Thirteenth century theologian, St. Thomas Aquinas, spent years trying to know God through rational defenses of Christian doctrine. His works filled multiple volumes with his thoughts and reasoning. But once he attained conscious contact with God, through the meditative process, he stopped writing. When asked why, he said that what he had been shown in meditation makes everything he had written, "*seem only as straw!*"

# Part VI.

# REAL VALUE
# OF THE PROGRAM

# DISCOVERING
# YOUR TRUE IDENTITY

$O$ne of the remarkable things you will discover, when you *awaken* to who you really are, is that your life will be filled with joy, happiness and freedom. Not just fleeting glimpses, but the daily sustainable experience of a deep and profound *knowing-feeling* that you are one of God's children, and, as such, you possess all of the blessings that you were endowed with in the beginning

If you are not fully experiencing this reality, your true identity has not yet been *uncovered*, and you are encouraged to continue in your search. The admonition, "Seek you first the Kingdom of God, and all these things will be added onto you," was not an idol promise. It has been fulfilled in the lives of many that have gone before you, who, just like you and me, had no idea that such feelings of joy, happiness and freedom were even possible, let alone available to them.

I'm reminded of the story of the search for the missing Maltese Falcon statue, which was made of pure gold. Apparently the person who stole the Falcon covered it with ordinary clay so that it could be smuggled out of the country

95

undetected. The scheme unraveled, however, when the statue was accidentally banged against another object and a chip of the clay came free, revealing that the clay was covering the solid gold Maltese Falcon.

This story strikes me as a perfect metaphor for our experience in this world. We would like to think that we're more valuable, but are unable to appreciate who we really are, because, over the years, we've covered our "golden reality" with so much "clay." On occasion we may have had a glimpse of our true identity, when we brushed up against something and exposed a small piece of the "gold." For just a brief moment, we experienced a sense of joy, happiness and freedom, like nothing we had felt before. We were convinced, at that moment, that there really was a God, and that all was right with the world! However, it didn't last, as the spot would be quickly covered over with more "clay," and we would once again lose sight of our true identity.

Our task is to unravel the scheme by discovering our true identity once and for all. Because, when we find out who we really are, we'll find the *sustainable* joy, happiness and freedom that we've been looking for!

# OPENING
# UNSEEN DOORS

Having allowed God into your life, you'll soon realize that he goes before you and prepares the way. And, that he can open "doors" you don't even know are there. When you undertake a mission with God, all he asks is that you believe in his capabilities; go right to the end of your "vision," and be willing to take the next step in faith. He'll take it from there!

Most of us used to see a huge wall ahead and complain that there was no way to proceed, as the wall was too high! No matter how much we prayed to have a door appear, so that we could pass through, nothing happened. What we failed to realize, was that God saw no reason to provide us with a door, let alone to open it, as we were nowhere near the wall. We were looking at the problem from a distance. As we weren't at the wall, why would we need a door? We're not ready to pass through, we're just *thinking* about it. We still have a distance to go. We need to go right up to the wall before there's any need for a door!

You will recall the allegorical story of Moses, where he was leading the Children of Israel in their exodus from Egypt, ahead of the pursuing army of the Pharaoh. He sent scouts ahead to find a way out, but they returned with the bad news of a huge sea that was blocking their way. They said there was no choice but to turn around, go back, and try to find another way. However, this was not a viable option, as to do so would have meant certain death to all at the hands of the Pharaoh's army.

Moses insisted that God had promised to deliver them, and would do so, if they trusted him and went forward in faith. They did. And, just as soon as Moses and his people arrived at the waters edge, the sea parted, and not a moment before. As why would the sea need to part if Moses and his people were not yet there? God's funny that way. He seems to insist that he will open doors only for those who have gone right up to the wall, confident that a door will be there and opened for them. The others don't need a door!

If you have defined your God with this capability, and are willing to go forward in faith, your path will be made clear, or a "door" will open that you didn't even know was there. What a wonderful thing to know as you begin each new day.

# STANDING
# ON A ROCK

Once you have discovered who you really are, you'll be overwhelmed by a tremendous sense of *gratitude!* Not just for the joy, happiness and freedom that is in your daily life, but for the knowledge that, in knowing who you are, you also know, by extension, who everybody else is!

You have become aware that most people, just like you and me, think that their life is separate and apart from all others. And that each one of them, just like you and me, has constructed a history about their respective lives and experiences, which they hold to be true. They will not only insist that that is who they are, but will protect the image even in the face of evidence to the contrary. It's as though their responses to life have been placed on "automatic pilot," to reflect *prior* navigational experience, without recognizing the *present* reality.

It's what is known as our "Ego-Self," or "First Voice" in spiritual dialogue. In point-of-fact, it's only our *conditioned mind's* first response to anything we encounter. And it's based on all that has gone before. The sum total of each past decision made to rationalize both the experience and our chosen response to it. It's all the "stuff" from which we have built both our personal identity and our so-called "reality." And we're stuck with it, until we find out who we *really* are!

We now understand why people hold the positions and beliefs that they do. It's their "reality story." And, it's a story that they're more than happy to defend against anybody else's "reality story." It can fuel some pretty serious arguments, particularly over who's *right* and who's *wrong*. Isn't it comforting to know that one is neither right nor wrong. It's just their conditioned response pronouncing on the event, as they perceive it from their personal perspective. However, the truth is, the facts of any situation are just the facts of the situation. Each individual is then free to respond to them in whatever way he or she feels is appropriate to accommodate their belief system. And they do!

Knowing that you're now trying to meet life with your "Second Voice" further extends your gratitude. This is the one that's heard only if you've allowed your First Voice to be "neutered," preventing it from "jumping" all over whatever you're confronted with. This Second Voice is your "Spiritual-Self," which is not motivated by your past experience, but rather from the newfound awareness of your spiritual reality and intuitive understanding of the *present* moment.

The difference in approach by these two voices is remarkable! Not only in content and direction, but also in the comfort and authority with which your Second Voice speaks. For this is the Voice that is being inspired by the "Source" of all knowledge, who knows precisely what needs to be done, or said, to best position you for what is next required to happen in your life. You're definitely going to have a better day using your Second Voice.

Your feelings of gratitude and confidence are further enhanced each day, because you have asked your God to help you to know what to do, and to give you the strength, power and ability to carry it out, in each and every encounter. You also know that he goes before you and prepares the way, and can open "doors" you don't even know are there. When these confidences are added to your knowledge that the Power behind you is far greater than the task ahead, your whole attitude and demeanor turn positive, and good things happen to you. Is it any wonder that you feel as though you're *standing on a rock?*

# SPIRITUAL VISION

Rose-coloured glasses have *nothing* on "spiritual vision." All that rose-coloured glasses do is *tint* what you're looking at with a rosy hue, making the image appear more pleasant to the eye. Whereas "spiritual vision" can diametrically change your perception of an event, or completely remove an unacceptable image from your conscious awareness. This phenomenon is just *one* of the blessings you will receive as a direct result of your newfound spiritual awakening.

An example of "spiritual vision," on a personal note, is what I experienced in my early thirties when I was struggling with what can best be described as an increasing reliance on alcohol in my search for "happiness." When I finally turned the whole matter over to God, and discovered a joy and happiness far greater than I was ever able to achieve through the use of alcohol, I quit drinking altogether. However, as important as that event was, and is, in my life, it only serves as the *backdrop* to the "spiritual vision" part of the story.

What I discovered, much to my surprise and delight, was that not only did I not need to use alcohol to enjoy my life, but that it had been "removed" from my conscious awareness! Whether it was in a social situation, or after a round of golf, if you asked me later who was drinking and who wasn't I couldn't really tell you. So, unless someone drew my attention to it by spilling a drink, or searching for a coaster, I was not consciously aware of its presence. Alcohol had disappeared from my "sight." And it's been that way for all these many years.

The same thing is true for smoking. I smoked for over twenty years. Then, after many unsuccessful attempts to quit on my own, I finally asked God to help me. He did, and I haven't smoked since. And, just like alcohol, smoking was *removed* from my sight! It's only if somebody is fussing over an ashtray, or fumbling for a match, that it catches my attention. Otherwise, I'm completely unaware of it. Talk about miracles!

You'll also notice that you "see" far fewer disappointments, now that you're allowing God to lead the way. That's mainly the result of being less inclined to set *expectations* for outcomes, for which you are not responsible. Your responsibility is for *inputs*, not *outcomes*. Therefore, if you're anticipating a certain result from a planned event, and it turned out differently, your attitude of "outcome acceptance" will automatically surface, negating the potential for disappointment. This allows you to still have a great day, even though your agenda has been overtaken by events *beyond* your immediate control. In fact, if you're anything like me, you'll probably find it somewhat *exciting* to watch what it is that comes into your life as a result of the revised agenda. Trust God, and watch what happens!

Your observations will also change through *seeing* many other things differently than you did before. "Spiritual vision" looks only upon "Life" in all that it beholds. Whether it's the budding of a flower in spring, or a funeral procession, the "good" is always recognized over the "bad" and the "ugly." And the "death" of anything is *seen* simply as an end to its present form, and a return to "Source."

Experience with this phenomenon goes far beyond these examples. However, I believe that they serve to demonstrate how "spiritual vision" can diametrically change what you "see" in your life. As your spiritual reality is further uncovered, you'll experience an increasing number of similar transformations, and recognize the incredible power that's working in your best interest, as God leads the way!

# Part VII.

# SHARED EXPERIENCES

# POETIC
# PROGRESSION

Over the past many years, one of the things I've enjoyed doing, is to sit down, in a quiet moment, and write something. This activity generally took place around the Christmas holidays, after I had wrapped up my business for the current year and was taking some personal time with my family.

During these reflective times, I would review the accomplishments of the past year and contemplate what the next year might bring. Invariably my thoughts would turn to gratitude for the many blessings that I was enjoying, not only in my business, or with my wife and family, but also in the continued *unfolding* of my awareness as to the *meaning* of life.

Religious teachings offer the names of several people credited with having experienced their "spiritual awakening" through what is described as a moment of "intense light," as in the conversion of Paul on the road to Damascus, or a "burning bush," in the case of Moses on Mt. Sinai. In that holy instant, God *revealed* himself to them, and their lives were changed completely, and forever.

That was *not* what happened to me. My spiritual awakening was what is commonly referred to as, "the educational variety." This type of awakening is the result of an extended series of learning experiences, and more modest revelations, which you subsequently recognize as having entered, and altered, your awareness.

This gradual *enlightenment* is reflected in my writings over the last thirty years, some of which I have included here, as I believe they are germane to our discussion. The time period covered by these writings is 1976 through 1983. That's when I first recognized that significant progress was being made in my spiritual awareness.

The first of the writings, "If You're Talking to Me," is a 1976 poem describing my willingness to "hear" from God, so that I too would be a "lover that's heard." Then in 1978 I found myself writing about my "Gifts to God," which represents a rather clear demonstration of turning my will and my life over to the care of God, as I understood him. At the same time I wrote "Thy Kingdom Come," capturing the wonderful feeling of my awareness that the Lord's Prayer had been *answered* in my life. Then, in 1983, the whole process of *returning* to God was made clear to me in the metaphorical "Come and be a Christmas Tree." Thank You God!

# "IF YOU'RE
# TALKING TO ME"

They say that you love me, and I believe that it's so.
But if you don't tell me, then how will I know?
I know you could tell me, without speaking a word.
Then I too would be a lover that's heard.

If you're talking to me, I can't hear you.
Please say it out loud, though I'm near you.
For I want to see all the beauty in thee,
And lose any reason to fear you.

You told others you loved them, then set them free.
Still they seem so convinced, that you truly love me.
They're beautiful people, and wouldn't be lying.
If I were to hear you, it would help me keep trying.

If you're talking to me, I can't hear you.
Please say it out loud, though I'm near you.
For I want to see all the beauty in thee,
And lose any reason to fear you.

# THROUGH THE EYE OF A NEEDLE

If your love has conditions, I'll follow the rules.
Your word spoken softly will furnish the tools.
To hear that you love me, would settle my grief,
And turn into knowledge, what is only belief.

If you're talking to me, I can't hear you.
Please say it out loud, though I'm near you.
For I want to see all the beauty in thee,
And lose any reason to fear you.

Not knowing the truth leaves so much in doubt.
Just one word from you, would straighten things out.
So please end my searching, and allow me to hear,
That you really do love me, and will always be near.

If you're talking to me, I can't hear you.
Please say it out loud, though I'm near you.
For I want to see all the beauty in thee,
And lose any reason to fear you.

# "GIFTS TO GOD"

## (Gold, Frankincense and Myrrh)

YOU knew the many ways I had tried to find happiness and a sense of purpose in my life. I tried to gain recognition through success in business, security through the gathering of possessions and peace of mind through the avoidance of conflict.

YOU also knew that these individual pursuits would work against the accomplishment of my objectives. Yet you allowed me to continue, for as long as I could, so that I too would know.

YOUR blessing of awareness has changed me. I now enjoy the fruit of your grace, without the need to give up or to deny myself anything. I let all things happen in your perfect order, which has always been, and always will be, in my best interest. I know who I am, where I came from and where I'm going. I stand on a rock, comfortable in the presence of all others and confident in the knowledge that I belong. I am free from fear and apprehension, and filled with faith and trust in your divine purpose. There truly is life eternal.

# THROUGH THE EYE OF A NEEDLE

YOU gave me all of this and more, and more, and more each day, when I came to you sincerely, and humbly offered my gifts of Gold, Frankincense and Myrrh:

GOLD – I gave you all of my possessions. Everything that I owned, had use of, or came into contact with, I gave over to you, to do with according to your will. My money, house, business, talents, family and best friends I recognize as belonging to you. You ask only that I do the best I can with each one of them.

FRANKINCENSE – I dedicated my life to you, and to your purpose. My morning prayer is only to know your will for me, and to have the strength, power and ability to carry it out. You have always gone before me to prepare the way. You ask only that I follow with faith and trust.

MYRRH – I gave to you, and you alone, the right to judge the motives and results for actions taken by my fellow man, no matter how adverse the consequences may appear. You have shown me that forgiveness and compassion immediately follow the recognition of truth. You ask only that I try.

## Reflection

"You will know them by their fruit." What fruit are you enjoying? Are you comfortable with your life? Are you truly happy each and every day, no matter what the circumstances? Do you have peace of mind and a sense of belonging? Are you confident in all situations, free of fear and apprehension? Are you filled with faith and trust in a Divine Purpose? Do you know that you have eternal life? If you have all of these things, continue to do what you're doing. If you do not enjoy every one of these blessings, then change what you're doing.

You don't have to wait for Christmas to offer your gifts of Gold, Frankincense and Myrrh to God, as you understand him. *Unless you want to!*

# "THY KINGDOM COME"

## (When the Lord's Prayer is Answered)

Creator of all things, your presence is everywhere,
    and awareness of you brings fulfilment.
When I came to know you, and the reality
    of my own existence,
My actions, here on earth, freely followed your will,
    as all in Heaven do.
Since finding your Kingdom, you've provided all
    of my needs, and I know that you always will.
I no longer sit in judgement of my fellow man,
    as I know that his actions are part of your plan.
This same knowledge has removed my feelings
    of guilt, resentment and remorse.
Being at one with you, in your Kingdom, I am
    not led into temptation, and
Evil has no place in the lives of people
    touched by your Holy Spirit.

# THROUGH THE EYE OF A NEEDLE

For you are the Power and the Glory
      that created all things for good.
It has always been this way, it is this way now,
      it will always be this way.
I am so grateful to know that I am part of you
      and your Kingdom, forever and ever. Amen.

# "COME AND BE A CHRISTMAS TREE"

Winter is cold and so unforgiving,
When you are a tree in wilderness living.
A spectator of life from season to season,
You can't but wonder if there's really a reason.

If you only knew what you're meant to be,
A reflection of Christ as a Christmas Tree.
So come forward now and be born anew,
Be freed from the roots that are binding to you.

Come live in his house with his full protection,
Enjoying the warmth of love and affection.
Then you'll be changed from imperfect and scorned,
To a vision of beauty so fully adorned.

Your branches will be laden with gifts undeserving,
A new sense of purpose from him you are serving.
These gifts you will share so freely with others,
For all will be treated as sisters and brothers.

# THROUGH THE EYE OF A NEEDLE

Keeping nothing for self means everything gained,
An abundance of joy and fulfilment sustained.
There's no greater goal, no greater reward,
Than performing your mission as set by the Lord.

If you only knew what you're meant to be,
A reflection of Christ as a Christmas Tree.
So come forward now and be born anew,
Be freed from the roots that are binding to you.

Be what you were meant to be.
Come, and be a Christmas Tree!

# COACH'S
# CLOSING COMMENTS

The existence of God does not depend on your *belief* in him. But the fullness of your joy, happiness and freedom, during your time in this world, does!

Your search for your own reality will lead you to know that God created you and loves you, and that he protects your *reality* in eternity. When your body finishes the work you have assigned to it, you will leave it behind and continue as your "Original Self." Joining with all others in "Spiritual Oneness," as God's Son. So fear not! Your "Life," after the physical "death" of your body, is *not* in jeopardy. It never was, and it never will be. It's God's promise to his beloved child. Count on it!

The question is, "What do you want to happen while you're here?" You have been given the freedom to choose. Your "Spiritual-Self" was created with the fullness of joy, happiness and freedom from the beginning, which is yours to enjoy if you *choose* "Life." A decision for "Life" means that you wish to participate in all of the blessings that are your inheritance as a child of God, right *here* and right *now!* This decision allows you the opportunity to enjoy what is generally referred to as "Heaven on Earth," in the Judeo-Christian lexicon; "Enlightenment," in Buddhism; and "Nirvana," in Hinduism. You'll enjoy the bliss and excitement of living a joyous, happy and free life, with child-like *enthusiasm,* each and every day, in perpetual wonder as to who you really are!

Or, you can *choose* to live as a *self-reliant* individual, intent on *controlling* what happens in your life, and seeking to establish special relationships with people that will bring comfort to you, and meaning to your existence. With this choice comes not only the responsibility for scripting your own life, and *engineering* acceptable outcomes, but also for *judging* the intentions and activities of everybody else, as they relate to you and your chosen agenda. An awesome task. And then you die!

The real tragedy of the second choice is not the "And then you die" part, as when you do you'll be with God in all of your glory as his Son. It's that you'll *forfeit* all of the *real* joy of life that is available to you, each and every minute, of each and every day, while you're here!

There are two things which are certain. One, you *don't* have to die to be in "Heaven." And two, you *do* have to die to be in "Heaven." It just depends on the choice you make *here* and *now*! God blesses you.

# Part VIII.

# ADDENDUM

# GLOSSARY OF TERMS

If we're to have a fruitful conversation, on any subject, we should first *define* our terms. This is even more important if our topic is at all controversial, or subject in large part to ones own *belief* system and *personal* experiences. The following are some of the terms used throughout the book which I believe require definition.

## "GOD"

The Prime Source of all being and life; the Creator of all things; the one known as "Father," whose fatherhood was established through his "First Cause," creating his son, the "Effect" known as "the Christ" (or "Christos" in early Egyptian mythology); the one whose essence is pure spirit, permeating all creation; whose unity is the *state* of Heaven; and the one who is described simply as, "I am," for to add anything else to the statement would be to limit, by definition, that which is *without* limit.

Note: To avoid issues of religious sensitivity (see God, Religion and Gender), in the hope of keeping our *focus* on universal spiritual themes, I've used the word "God" throughout the book to represent most facets of that which is "Divine." Some readers might be more comfortable substituting the descriptive language of their personal religious beliefs.

## "SON OF GOD"

The *totality* of the Sonship of God; the "Effect" of the "First Cause;" the "Self" which God created by the extension of his spirit; known as "the Christ" (or "Christos" in early Egyptian mythology) who is our *true* self; and, is an *expression* of our unified relationship to God. It is the Son's function in Heaven to create, as it was God's in creating him.

## "HOLY SPIRIT"

The communication *link* between God and us, as his "separated" Son, allowing us to share the totality of his love; bridging the *gap* between the Mind of Christ and our "split-mind" (duality of spirit and separation); the one who leads us through our *illusions* to the truth; and, is the "Voice" of God, who speaks for him and for our spiritual-self, reminding us of our *true* identity, which we had forgotten.

## "HEAVEN"

The pre-separation world of God and his unified creation, *exclusive* of the world of *perception*; the perfect union of God's will and spirit; a *state* that can be reflected in the *here-now*, through a holy relationship with the *real* world; and, is the peaceful *knowing-feeling* that God is in his "Heaven" and all is "right" with the world.

# "SPIRITUAL- SELF"

The *changeless* and *eternal* spiritual nature of our true reality; in contra-distinction to the "Ego-Self," personified in our body, which *changes* and *dies*; the thought in God's mind, which is the unified Christ; and is our reality as *pure spirit* in the *image* of God, our Father.

# "EGO-SELF"

Our false "reality," created through "separation" from God to conduct our affairs in *ignorance* of his will for us; a substitute for the "Spiritual-Self" that God created; a thought system that gives rise to sin, guilt and fear; the "protector" of our separated *individuality*; and, the powerful personal motivating force, with no plan for success, only a never-ending drive for "more," to satisfy our *feelings* of need.

# "SPIRITUAL AWAKENING"

Waking from the "dream" of separation to the *reality* of who we really are; knowing that we live *here-now*, in *eternity*, as an integral part of the oneness we share in Christ; exceptionally aware of the joy, happiness and freedom that is ours, and has been from the beginning; recognizing that the "Holy Spirit" goes before us and prepares the way; and *communicating* with the world through our spiritual reality.

# INDEX

# MEMBERSHIP
# AND PROGRAM SUPPORT

## Membership:

Membership in The Spiritual Coach Program is simply a matter of registering with The Spiritual Coach at our web site, www.thespiritualcoach.net. Select the 'Electronic Outreach' page from the menu, fill in the contact information on the form provided, and press 'Send.' Membership is free.

As a registered Member, you are entitled to submit any questions that you may have about the program, by email, directly to the Coach. (Only registered Members may submit questions). Members also receive an email every week to share in the Coach's Weekly Message.

## Financial Support for the Program:

The Spiritual Coach Program relies entirely on the royalties from book sales, and the income generated from Speaking Engagements, Seminars, Retreats and Private Coaching, to cover all operating costs and program development expenses.

If you would like to engage the Coach to participate in a forthcoming event, or to arrange for Private Coaching, please contact us directly at coach@thespiritualcoach.net

## Ordering Additional Books:

Copies of "Through the Eye of a Needle" are available through most bookstores, or may be purchased directly from the Publisher by calling the Book Orders Hotline 888-280-7715, or over the internet at www.authorhouse.com.

# ABOUT
# THE AUTHOR

Stan Sanderson is the author of the book, founder of The Spiritual Coach™ and creator of The Spiritual Coach Program™. He studied the technique of Transcendental Meditation©, as taught by His Holiness Maharishi Mahesh Yogi, through the Internationasl Meditation Society, in the early 1970's. His personal spiritual experiences were confirmed in "A Course In Miracles®," which he has fully embraced. ACIM also helped inform his universal spiritual principles.

Over many years, Stan has used his personal experience and teaching skills to help others find the *happiness* they seek. He recently published an online website, *www.thespiritualcoach.net*, to provide an "Electronic Outreach" for participants and members of The Spiritual Coach Program.

Stan enjoyed successful careers in both the medical supply business and the financial services industry, before retiring from active business in 2001. He has been an industry leader in having served as both President and Chairman of the Board of Directors for the Canadian Association of Financial Planners (CAFP); and President of the Canadian Surgical Trade Association (CSTA).

His public service commitments included accepting an appointment by the Government of Ontario to serve as a Trustee, and subsequently as Chair of the Board of Trustees, for the Ontario Public Service Employees Union (OPSEU) Pension Plan. His biography is listed in the Canadian Who's Who.

Stan is married with four children and eight grandchildren. He and his wife, Elizabeth, recently moved from their family home in Oakville to the Villages of Leacock Point in Orillia, Ontario.